for
Elizabeth

The LETTERS are LOST!

Lisa Campbell Ernst

PUFFIN BOOKS

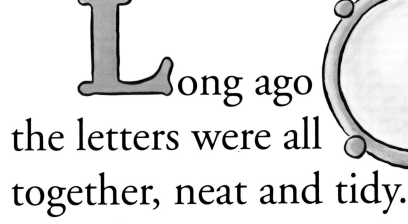

Long ago the letters were all together, neat and tidy.

But time passed. First one block disappeared, then the next, and the next, until now — their box is empty.

The letters are lost! Come, let's find them, one by one.

flew high in an Airplane.

tumbled into the Bath.

joined a family of Cows.

was a Dog's tasty toy.

found a home
with some Eggs.

took a swim
with the Fish.

G stopped to look
through some Glasses.

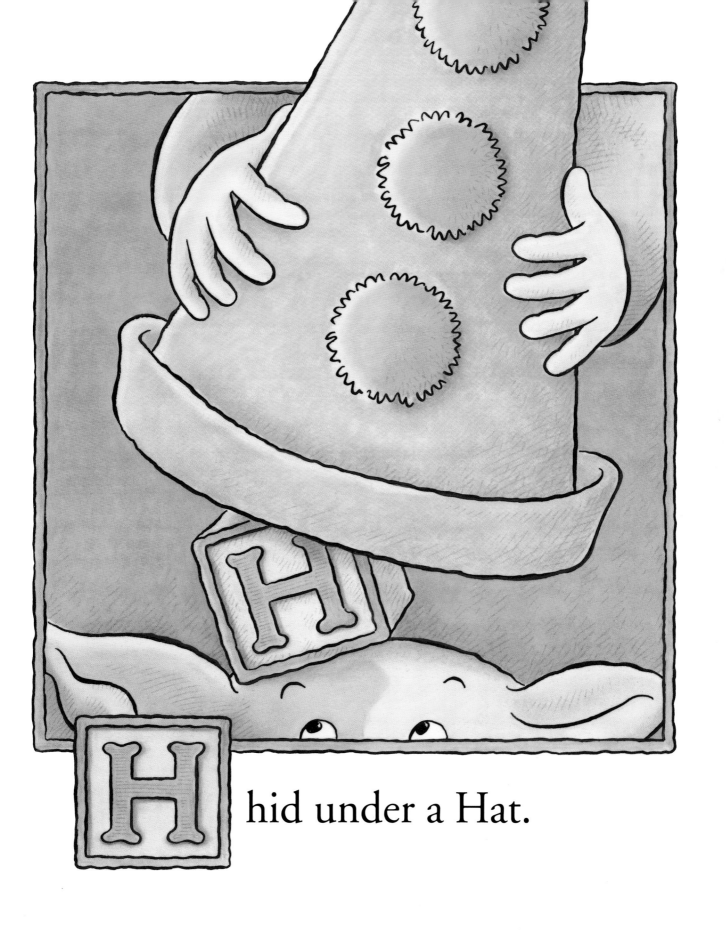

hid under a Hat.

I longed for strawberry Ice cream.

jumped out of a
Jack-in-the-box.

hitched a ride in a
Kangaroo pouch.

landed in a pile of Leaves.

admired himself
in a Mirror.

found a tower
of Numbers.

peeked through an Oval.

dove into the Popcorn.

took a nap on a Quilt.

R rolled away on
   a Roller skate.

S went to play
in the Sandbox.

helped to squish out
the Toothpaste.

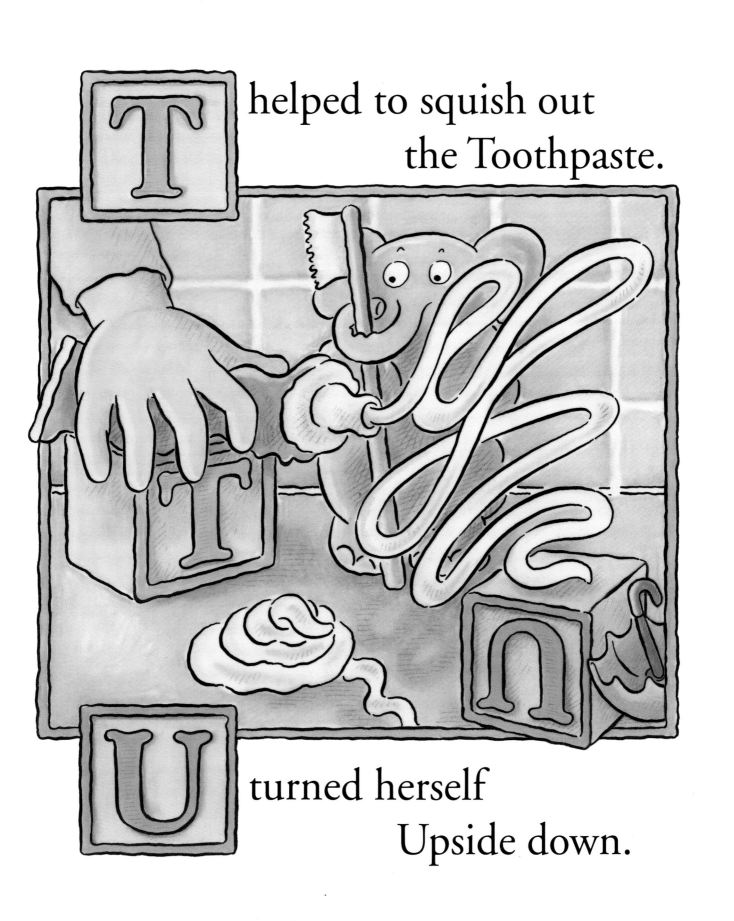

turned herself
Upside down.

V made a fancy Valentine.

W fell into the
Washing machine.

played the XYlophone.

did a jig with a Zebra.

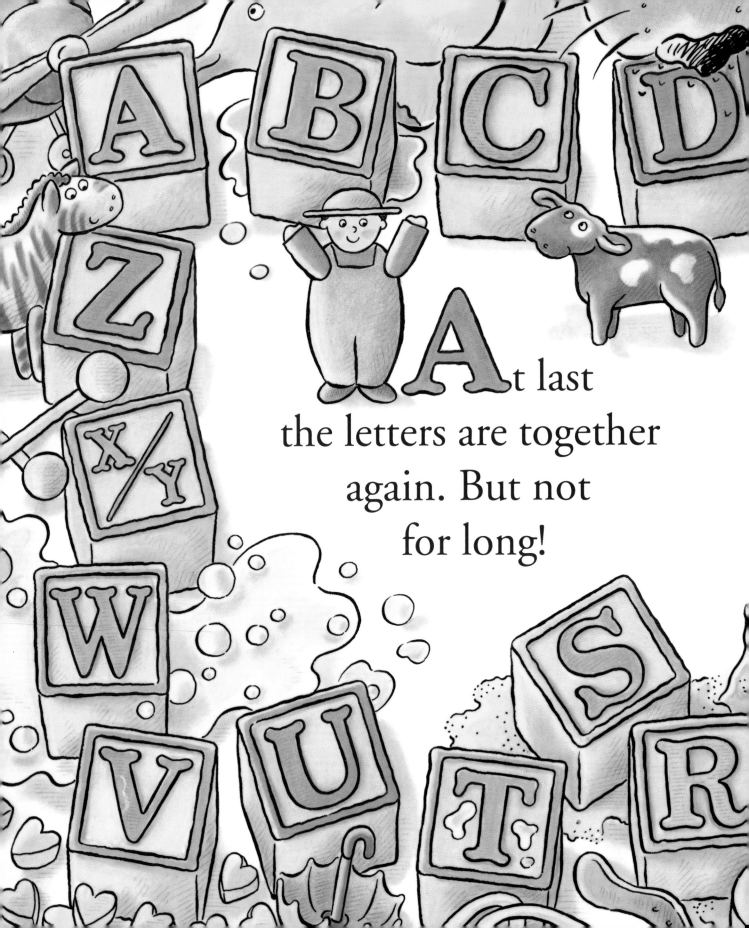

At last the letters are together again. But not for long!

Soon the blocks will begin to disappear once more. Can you guess where they might go?

PUFFIN BOOKS
Published by the Penguin Group
Penguin Putnam Books for Young Readers, 345 Hudson Street, New York, New York 10014, U.S.A.
Penguin Books Ltd, 27 Wrights Lane, London W8 5TZ, England
Penguin Books Australia Ltd, Ringwood, Victoria, Australia
Penguin Books Canada Ltd, 10 Alcorn Avenue, Toronto, Ontario, Canada M4V 3B2
Penguin Books (N.Z.) Ltd, 182-190 Wairau Road, Auckland 10, New Zealand

Penguin Books Ltd, Registered Offices: Harmondsworth, Middlesex, England

First published in the United States of America by Viking,
a division of Penguin Books USA Inc., 1996
Published by Puffin Books, a member of Penguin Putnam Books for Young Readers, 1999

10

Copyright © Lisa Campbell Ernst, 1996
All rights reserved

THE LIBRARY OF CONGRESS HAS CATALOGED THE VIKING EDITION AS FOLLOWS:
Ernst, Lisa Campbell.
The letters are lost! / [text and illustrations by] Lisa Campbell Ernst.
p.   cm.
Summary: Long ago all the letters of the alphabet were together in their box,
but one by one they disappeared and now the reader helps to find them.
ISBN 0-670-86336-X
[1. Lost and found possessions—Fiction. 2. Alphabet.]
I. Title.
PZ7.E7323Le 1996 [E]—dc20 95-42209 CIP AC

Puffin Books ISBN 0-14-055663-X

Manufactured in China